A CHRISTMAS CAROL

Adapted for Theater

Preface by GARLAND WRIGHT, *Artistic Director, The Guthrie Theater*

Illustrations by STEPHEN T. JOHNSON

A Donna Martin Book

ANDREWS AND McMEEL • KANSAS CITY

A Christmas Carol: Adapted for Theater by Donna Martin copyright © 1993 by Andrews and McMeel.
Illustrations copyright © 1993 by Stephen T. Johnson

Library of Congress Cataloging-in-Publication Data

Martin, Donna, 1935–
A Christmas carol / adapted for theater by Donna Martin ;
preface by Garland Wright ; illustrations by Stephen T. Johnson.
p.   cm.
"A Donna Martin book."
Summary: Presents, in prose form, the stage adaptation
of the famous story in which the
miserly Scrooge learns the true meaning of Christmas.
ISBN 0-8362-4507-5 : $14.95
[1. Christmas—Fiction. 2. Ghosts—Fiction. 3. England—Fiction.]
I. Johnson, Stephen, 1964–   ill. II. Dickens, Charles, 1812–1870.
Christmas carol. III. Title.
PZ7.M356818Ch   1993
[Fic]—dc20   93-14679
                                                                       CIP
                                                                        AC

Book design by Rick Cusick
Typeset by Connell-Zeko
Printed by Tien Wah Press

A Christmas Carol by Charles Dickens was first published on December 19, 1843. Ten years later, Dickens himself gave the first public reading from the book. Dickens, who had seriously considered an acting career as a young man, offered to do a reading in public as a benefit for a charitable organization. Two thousand people, assembled in the Town Hall of Birmingham, England, cheered the famous author.

But the idea of performing *A Christmas Carol* on stage was not the author's alone. In New York City, a year after its publication, the first American stage production of *A Christmas Carol* opened at the Park Theatre to disastrous reviews. After that, it was not performed again in America until 1867, when Dickens gave a reading to an audience in Tremont Temple, Boston. From then on it became an American custom to give public readings from the book at Christmas. Today, perhaps the most widely acclaimed one-man show is by actor Patrick Stewart.

A Christmas Carol had its first of numerous screen adaptations in 1901. *Scrooge, or Marley's Ghost,* a one-reel silent feature, was produced in England but never shown in America. What followed were several early American silent film versions, produced in 1908, 1911, 1916, and 1922. The first major American film, an MGM production starring Reginald Owen, came in 1938. Lionel Barrymore, known for reading the play on radio in the 1930s, was prevented by illness from being cast in the movie. Perhaps the most famous English film was the 1951 production starring Alastair Sim. Other screen productions include a musical starring Albert Finney, released in 1970, and Michael Caine's turn as Scrooge in *The Muppets Christmas Carol,* released in 1992. Memorable television performances include the first color production, starring Fredric March as Scrooge and Basil Rathbone as Marley in 1954, and a CBS television movie starring George C. Scott, which premiered in 1984.

The 1970s brought a resurgence of stage performances in American regional theaters. One of the first productions appeared at the Guthrie Theater in Minneapolis in 1975. Adapted by Barbara Field and still performed today, this production features an actor who plays Dickens. Cajoled by his family to join them for the Christmas pudding, he is instead intent upon finishing *A Christmas Carol* and opens and closes the play as its narrator. This production has been used or adapted by numerous other theater companies, including Kansas City's Missouri Repertory Theatre, in which costumed characters mingle with the audience before the performance and sing carols in the lobby afterward.

In the Guthrie performance, a few elements have been added for theatrical purposes: Scrooge throws a paperweight at his nephew, a paperweight that resurfaces in several scenes as a reminder of a bond of affection that Scrooge once had and lost. Another scene features the young Ebenezer in the schoolyard, rather than alone with his books at school. His sister Fan comes, not to take him home (to be apprenticed in three days, as in the story) but to apologize that Father will not allow him to come home, giving viewers some insight into his deprived childhood. The playgoer also meets Belle in an early scene just before Scrooge is apprenticed to Mr. Fezziwig, putting her later "release" of Scrooge from their marriage contract into context. The adaptation in this book includes these elements of the Guthrie version.

More than fifty professional theaters and hundreds of community and amateur theaters now perform *A Christmas Carol* annually. Children love to attend these performances, to be frightened by the Ghost of Marley as he rises out of the trap door in a waft of smoke, and to share the joy of Tiny Tim's recovery, thanks to the reformation of Ebenezer Scrooge. This version serves to make the theatrical performance a little easier to follow, while preserving much of the original dialogue of Dickens's inspired and beloved story.

GARLAND WRIGHT
Artistic Director, The Guthrie Theater

A Christmas Carol

THERE'S MANY FINE FOLKS WHO SPEND CHRISTMAS EVE DECORATING THEIR TREE AND BUYING AND WRAPPING GRAND GIFTS TO GO UNDER IT. THEN THERE WERE KIDS LIKE ME, WHO WERE TOO POOR TO EXPECT A FEAST ON CHRISTMAS DAY, BUT WE KEPT THE SPIRIT ANYWAY. Out on the streets there was so much merriment and good will that you almost forgot how cold it was! Everybody, rich and poor alike, would wish each other a Merry Christmas, and even the fine ladies and gentlemen would stop to hear a carol, and sometimes sing along! Everybody but Scrooge, that is.

This is the story of that man, Mr. Ebenezer Scrooge, the surviving partner of the firm of Scrooge and Marley, and how he came to keep Christmas Day. I know this story in part firsthand, because I knew the very beginning and the ending, which I will share with you. As you will come to understand, I learned the rest—about his miraculous transformation—from Mr. Scrooge himself. For a boy like me to have had a part in it was the most wonderful Christmas gift I have ever had! It started, you see, with Mr. Scrooge right there on the street, bustling his way to the office, hurrying past the carolers, responding to every wish of "Merry Christmas!" with a nasty reply: "Bah, humbug!" I always wondered why he was so mean tempered, even though he was known to be one of the wealthiest men in town, but he didn't dampen my spirits any.

The streets were so filled with singing and dancing, juggling and joking, and kindness spilled out of every hand, sometimes in the form of a piece of fruit or a coin pressed into our cold palms.

But Scrooge went past us into his counting house, where poor Bob Cratchit had the misfortune to work for him as a clerk. Mr. Cratchit had to wear his overcoat at the office and warm his hands by the candle he copied by, because Mr. Scrooge was very stingy with coal to replenish the fire. It was, therefore, into a very bleak room that Mr. Scrooge's nephew opened the door one Christmas Eve.

"A Merry Christmas, Uncle!" he said. "God save you!"

"Bah!" said Scrooge. "Humbug!"

But Scrooge's nephew had, like the rest of us, heated himself with the exercise of walking, and his eyes sparkled and his breath smoked.

"Christmas a humbug, Uncle!" said Scrooge's nephew. "You don't mean that, I am sure?"

"I do," said Scrooge. "Merry Christmas! What reason have you to be merry? You're poor enough."

"Come, then," said the nephew gaily. "What right have you to be dismal? You're rich enough!"

Scrooge, having no better answer ready, said, "Bah!" again, and followed it up with "Humbug!"

"Don't be cross, Uncle," said the nephew.

"What else can I be," said the Uncle, "when I live in such a world of fools as this? Merry Christmas! What's Christmastime to you but a time for paying bills without money; a time for finding yourself a year older and not an hour richer? Keep Christmas in your own way and let me keep it in mine!"

"Keep it!" repeated Scrooge's nephew. "But you don't keep it at all!"

"Leave me alone, then. Much good may it do you! Much good it has ever done you!"

"There are many things which have done me good, from which I have

not profited," replied the nephew, "Christmas among them. But I have always thought of Christmastime, when it has come 'round, as a good time: a kind, forgiving, charitable, pleasant time. And therefore, Uncle, even though it has never put a scrap of gold or silver in my pocket, I believe that it has done me good, and will do me good; and I say, God bless it!"

Without meaning to, Bob Cratchit applauded, and then, suddenly self-conscious, poked at the fire and extinguished the last spark.

"Come dine with us tomorrow!" said the nephew.

Scrooge said emphatically that he would not.

"But why?" cried Scrooge's nephew. "Why?"

"Why did you get married?" asked Scrooge.

"Because I fell in love."

"Because you fell in love," growled Scrooge, as if that were the only thing in the world more ridiculous than a merry Christmas. "Good afternoon."

"I'll keep my Christmas humor to the last," said the nephew. "So a Merry Christmas! And a Happy New Year!"

At this, Scrooge grew so angry he threw a glass paperweight at his nephew, who caught it skillfully. "Why, thank you for the gift, Uncle!" he said.

As he left, Scrooge's nephew offered his greetings to Bob Cratchit, who, cold as he was, was warmer than Scrooge, for he returned them cordially.

This set Scrooge to muttering, for his clerk, making fifteen shillings a week, with a wife and a family, had even less reason to celebrate Christmas! And what's more, in letting his nephew out, Bob Cratchit had let two other people in! Would there be no end to the interruptions?

The new visitors were portly gentlemen. They took off their hats, books and papers in hand, and bowed to him. One of them was hard-of-hearing and held an ear trumpet.

"Scrooge and Marley's, I believe," said the other. "Do I have the pleasure of addressing Mr. Scrooge, or Mr. Marley?"

"Mr. Marley's been dead for seven years," Scrooge replied. "He died seven years ago this very night."

"We have no doubt he is generously represented by his partner," said the gentleman, presenting his card.

Scrooge frowned and shook his head, handing the card back. "At this festive season of the year, Mr. Marley," said the gentleman with the ear trumpet, "you will surely want to help provide for the poor and destitute, who suffer greatly at this time."

The first gentleman gently hushed his companion. "Many thousands are in want of common necessities, Mr. Scrooge," he said. "Hundreds of thousands are in need of the common comforts, sir."

"Are there no prisons?" asked Scrooge.

"Plenty of prisons," said the gentleman.

"And the workhouses?" said Scrooge. "Are they still in operation?"

"They are still," returned the gentleman. "I wish I could say they were not."

"Oh! I was afraid from what you said at first that something had occurred to stop them in their useful operation."

"Because they scarcely furnish Christmas cheer," returned the gentleman, "a few of us are trying to raise a fund to buy the poor some meat and drink and means of warmth. We choose this time because it is a time, above all others, when want is keenly felt while others rejoice in their abundance. How much can I put you down for?"

"Nothing!" Scrooge replied.

"You wish to remain anonymous, Mr. Marley?" the gentleman with the ear trumpet asked.

"I am Scrooge and I wish to be left alone! I can't afford to make idle people merry. My taxes help to support the establishments I mentioned. Those who are badly off can go there."

"Many can't go there," said the first gentleman, "and many would rather die."

"If they had rather die," said Scrooge, "they had better do it, and decrease the surplus population. Good afternoon, gentlemen!"

"But Mr. Marley!" cried the gentleman with the ear trumpet as his colleague hurried him out.

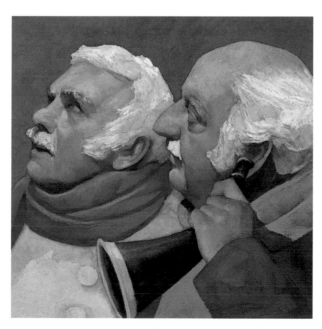

Eventually it came time to close the office. In foul humor, Scrooge dismounted from his stool, signaling to his expectant clerk that he could snuff his candle out.

"You'll want the whole day off tomorrow, I suppose?" said Scrooge.

"If it's quite convenient, sir."

"It's not convenient," said Scrooge.

"But Christmas comes only once a year, sir," said the clerk.

"A poor excuse for picking a man's pocket every twenty-fifth of December!" said Scrooge, buttoning his coat to his chin. "But I suppose you must have the whole day. Be here earlier than usual the next morning!"

"Oh, I will, sir!" said Bob Cratchit. "And Merry Christmas, sir!" Seeing Scrooge's frown, Bob hastily wrapped his thin cape and scarf around him and rushed out the door. Scrooge ate his usual dinner in a dim and dismal tavern, passing the evening by checking over his accounts. Then he went home to his gloomy apartment, growling at those along the way who wished him cheer. It was now so dark that Scrooge had to grope his way through the yard to his door.

Now there was nothing particular about the knocker on that door except that it was very large. Scrooge had seen it night and morning the whole time he had lived there. Nor had Scrooge given any thought to Marley since the mention of his name in the offices that afternoon. How strange it was, then, that Scrooge, having placed his key in the lock of the door, saw before him, not a knocker but Marley's face! As Scrooge looked intensely at this sight, it turned into a door knocker again. He studied the knocker a moment longer and saw nothing else, so he closed the door with a bang.

He locked the door and walked through the hall and up the stairs. In his bedroom, he slipped into his nightshirt. After placing his nightcap on his head, he started to blow out the candle so he could go to sleep. Suddenly he heard a clanking noise.

As Scrooge descended the stairs, the cellar door flew open with a booming sound and then, much louder, a kind of groan. Emerging from a terrible

burst of smoke was a fearsome sight: a ghost! It was the scariest thing you can imagine! His face was ashen white, and the chain he drew was clasped around his waist and wound about him like a tail. On it hung cashboxes, keys, padlocks, and heavy purses made of steel.

"Who are you?" asked Scrooge, terrified.

"Ask me who I was."

"Who were you, then?" said Scrooge, raising his voice.

"In life I was your partner, Jacob Marley."

"Can you—can you sit down?" asked Scrooge doubtfully.

"I can."

"Do it, then."

"You don't believe in me," observed the Ghost.

"I don't," said Scrooge.

"Why do you doubt your senses?"

"Because," said Scrooge, "a little thing can affect them. You may be an undigested bit of beef, a blot of mustard, a crumb of cheese, a fragment of an underdone potato. Humbug, I say, humbug!"

At this the Spirit raised a frightful cry and shook its chain with such an appalling noise that Scrooge held on tightly to his chair to keep from fainting. Then Scrooge fell upon his knees and clasped his hands before his face.

"Mercy!" he cried. "Dreadful apparition, why are you bothering me?"

"It is required of every man," the Ghost replied, "that his spirit should mingle with and enrich his fellow men and travel far and wide; and if that spirit goes not forth in life, it is condemned to do so after death. It is doomed to wander through the world and witness what it cannot share, but might have shared on earth, and turned to happiness!"

"You are in chains," said Scrooge. "Tell me why?"

"I wear the chain I forged in life," replied the Ghost. "I made it link by link and yard by yard. Is its pattern unfamiliar to you? The chain you bear

yourself was as heavy and as long as this seven Christmas Eves ago. And you have labored on it since. It is a heavy chain!"

"Jacob," Scrooge said imploringly, "say something comforting to me."

"I have no comfort to give," the Ghost replied. "A very little more is permitted me. I cannot rest, I cannot linger anywhere. In life my spirit never moved beyond the narrow limits of our money-changing hole; and weary journeys lie before me! No regret can make amends for one's life's opportunity misused!"

"But you were always a good businessman, Jacob," observed Scrooge, applying this virtue to himself.

"Business!" cried the Ghost, shaking its chains fearfully. "I should have known that mankind was my business. The common welfare was my business. Charity, mercy, forbearance, and benevolence were all my business. The dealings of our trade were but a drop of water in the ocean of my business! Hear me! My time is nearly gone."

"I will!" said Scrooge. "But don't be hard on me, Jacob."

"I am here to warn you that you have tonight one more chance and hope of escaping my fate. A chance and hope I have procured for you, Ebenezer."

"You were always a good friend to me," said Scrooge. "Thank you!"

"You will be haunted," continued the Ghost, "by three spirits."

"Is that the chance and hope you mentioned, Jacob?" he asked, in a faltering voice.

"It is."

"I—I think I'd rather not," said Scrooge.

"Without their visits," said the Ghost, "you cannot hope to avoid the path I tread. Expect the first tomorrow, when the bell tolls twelve."

"Couldn't they come all at once, and get it over with, Jacob?" hinted Scrooge.

"Expect the second on the next night at the same hour. The third upon the next night when the last stroke of twelve has ceased. Look to see no more of me, and for your own sake, remember what has passed between us!"

The Ghost walked backward from him, holding up his hand, warning Scrooge to come no closer. Suddenly the Ghost had disappeared.

He tried to say "Humbug!" but stopped at the first syllable. And, from the emotion he had undergone and the lateness of the hour, Scrooge found himself in need of rest. He went straight to bed and fell asleep instantly.

SCROOGE AWOKE JUST AS THE CHIMES OF A NEIGH-
BORING CHURCH BEGAN TO STRIKE. TO HIS GREAT ASTONISH-
MENT THE HEAVY BELL STRUCK TWELVE. But it was past two when he
went to bed. The clock was wrong! Twelve!

Suddenly a light flashed up in the room and the curtains of his bed were
drawn aside by a hand. Scrooge, sitting up, found himself face-to-face with an
unearthly visitor.

It was a strange figure. The hair which hung down its back was white as
if with age, and yet the face was like a child's. It wore a tunic of the purest
white, and round its waist was bound a belt, the sheen of which was beautiful.
From the crown of its head there sprung a bright clear jet of light, by which all
this was visible.

"Are you the Spirit whose coming was foretold to me?" asked Scrooge.

"I am!"

"Who and what are you?" Scrooge demanded.

"I am the Ghost of Christmas Past."

"Long past?" inquired Scrooge.

"No. Your past."

Scrooge then asked what business brought the Spirit there.

"Your welfare!" said the Ghost.

Scrooge said he was much obliged, but could not help thinking that a
good night's sleep would have been better.

"Your salvation, then. Take heed!" It put out its strong hand as it spoke,
and clasped Scrooge gently by the arm. "Rise and walk with me!"

It would have been in vain for Scrooge to plead that the weather and the
hour were not intended for such purposes, that he was dressed too lightly in his
nightgown and nightcap. The grasp was not to be resisted.

Together, to Scrooge's astonishment, they passed through the wall and
over the city and soon stood upon an open country road, with fields on either

side. The darkness had vanished, too, replaced by a clear, cold winter day.

"Good heavens!" said Scrooge, clasping his hands together as he looked about him. "This is where I grew up! I was a boy here!"

They walked along the road, Scrooge recognizing every gate and post and tree, until they came to a school yard. A little boy sat on a swing, all alone, sadly singing a Christmas carol. The other schoolboys had gone home.

"That little boy is me!" cried Scrooge, approaching.

"Yes," said the Spirit. "He cannot see you. These are but the shadows of the past."

Suddenly a little girl came from behind and covered his eyes with her hands, crying, "Merry Christmas, dear brother!"

"Why, Fan!" he cried, his voice suddenly lighting up.

"I have brought you a present," she said, taking from her pocket a paper-weight, the very one Scrooge threw at his nephew.

"Why, it's beautiful!" he said.

"I'm sorry Father will not allow you to come home for the holidays," she said. "But I sneaked away when he was busy. I wanted to see you. And to wish you a Merry Christmas."

"Thank you, Fan," he said, a little sadly.

"She was always a delicate creature," said the Ghost, "but she had a large heart!"

"So she had," said Scrooge.

"She grew up to be a good woman," said the Ghost, "and before she died, she had, I think, children."

"One child," Scrooge replied.

"True," said the Ghost. "Your nephew, who has not forgotten his mother's love!"

Suddenly they left the school behind them, and were now observing a young man pacing outside the doors of a party. A beautiful young woman approached him.

"You look uncomfortable," she remarked.

"And so I am," he replied. "I'm afraid I don't know party behavior."

"Nor do I," she said, smiling sweetly.

"I'm afraid I shall do something stupid, like use a fork for my soup."

"Or butter your tie!" she cried, laughing.

"But who are you?" he asked.

"Cinderella," she replied. "And tomorrow I shall return to sweeping the hearth!"

"No, really," he said.

"My name is Belle," she said, "and I am the governess to the children who live here."

"Ah, tomorrow I am to be apprenticed nearby, to Mr. Fezziwig," he replied. "Allow me to introduce myself. My name is Ebenezer Scrooge. And my beautiful Belle, I would like you to marry me!"

"Oh, but I have no dowry!" said Belle, laughing softly at his boldness.

"It doesn't matter!" said Scrooge. "For I intend to earn enough money to make us both very rich!"

"Well, we shall see!" said Belle, laughing. "We shall see!"

As the Spirit whisked Scrooge away from this scene, he looked back wistfully. Soon they were flying above the busy thoroughfares of a city. The Ghost stopped at a certain door and asked Scrooge if he knew it.

"Know it!" said Scrooge. "I was apprenticed here!"

They went in. At the sight of an old gentleman in a wig sitting behind a high desk, Scrooge cried in great excitement: "Why, it's old Fezziwig! Bless his heart. It's Fezziwig alive again!"

Mr. Fezziwig laid down his pen and looked up at the clock. "Yo ho, there! Ebenezer! Dick!"

Scrooge's former self, now a few years older than before, his face somewhat hardened by greed, came briskly in, accompanied by his fellow apprentice.

"That's Dick Wilkins!" said Scrooge to the Ghost. "Bless me, yes. He was very much attached to me."

"No more work tonight," said Fezziwig. "Christmas Eve, Dick. Christmas, Ebenezer! Let's close the shutters up!"

Everything movable was packed away, the floor was swept, wood was heaped upon the fire, and the office was transformed into a ballroom.

"Is Belle coming?" asked Dick Wilkins.

"Indeed she is," said Ebenezer, producing a ring from his pocket and showing it to Dick. "And tonight I intend to tell her I am ready to marry!"

Soon the room began to fill with merriment. In came a fiddler who began to play. In came Mrs. Fezziwig, a homely woman full of cheerfulness. In came the two Miss Fezziwigs, beaming and plain, clearly bent on winning their suitors tonight. In came other visitors, one after another, until there were enough to dance, and dance they did. Then Mr. Fezziwig, clapping his hands to stop the dance, cried "Well done!" He introduced his daughters, and it was clear that in his loving eyes, these plain young women were as beautiful as any on earth. As he announced their engagements, his eyes shone with pride and tears. Then, considerate as always, he turned to Ebenezer. "Why, where is Belle?" he asked.

"She's late," he frowned. "I'll have to speak to her about that."

There were more dances and there was cake and a great piece of cold roast and mince pies. But nothing matched the dancing of Mr. and Mrs. Fezziwig. Two portly people, they danced with a grace endowed by love. "Isn't he clever?" Mrs. Fezziwig was heard to say. "Isn't she beautiful?" he said to all around. And, indeed, although they were not handsome in any conventional sense, their affection and joy were contagious to all the guests.

Finally Ebenezer looked out to see Belle approaching the party. "You are late!" he said sharply.

"We need to talk, Ebenezer," she said, in tears.

"Yes, I had chosen this evening to tell you I believe I have achieved sufficient prosperity to allow us to complete our marriage contract," he replied.

"Our contract?" said Belle softly. "Ah, yes. You always speak in business terms. I'm sorry, Ebenezer, but another idol has displaced me. Perhaps it can cheer and comfort you in the time to come, as I would have tried to do."

"What idol has displaced you?" he asked.

"A golden one. I have seen your nobler aspirations disappear one by one, until only gain interests you. Have I not?"

"What then?" he replied. "Even if I have grown so much wiser now than then, I am not changed toward you."

She shook her head. "You have changed. When our contract, as you choose to call it, was made, you were another man."

"I was a boy," he said impatiently.

"I release you, Ebenezer," she said. "If you were free today, I do not believe you would choose to marry a poor girl—you who weigh everything by profit. I release you, with a heart full of love for the man you once were. May you be happy in the life you have chosen!"

She left him.

"Don't let her go!" cried Scrooge to his younger self.

But Ebenezer returned to the ball distraught and angry. When the clock struck eleven, the ball broke up. Mr. and Mrs. Fezziwig shook hands with the guests individually as they left and wished Ebenezer a Merry Christmas.

"Bah, humbug!" cried Ebenezer, and rushed through the door.

"Spirit," said Scrooge, "show me no more! Take me home. Haunt me no longer!"

Suddenly Scrooge was conscious of being overcome by drowsiness and, further, of being in his own bedroom. He barely had time to reel into bed before he sank into a heavy sleep.

Awakening again, Scrooge tried to collect his thoughts as the clock was once more on the stroke of twelve. When no shape appeared immediately, he felt confusion and a little disbelief. And then he saw a ghostly light and got up and shuffled to the door to trace it. Suddenly, a strange voice called to him to come down. He entered his own living room, no question about that, but it had undergone a surprising transformation. Above his fireplace were crisp leaves of holly, mistletoe, and ivy. Heaped upon a table were turkeys, geese, great joints of meat, suckling pigs, mince pies, plum puddings, chestnuts, apples, oranges, pears, and bowls of punch. Presiding over this table was a jolly giant, who bore a glowing torch, not unlike a horn of plenty.

"Come in!" exclaimed the giant. "Come in and know me better, little man!"

Scrooge entered timidly.

"I am the Ghost of Christmas Present," said the Spirit. "Look upon me!"

Scrooge did so. The Spirit was clothed in a deep green robe, bordered with white fur. On its head it wore a holly wreath.

"You have never seen the likes of me before!" exclaimed the Spirit.

"Never," said Scrooge. "Spirit," he added, "conduct me where you will."

"Touch my robe!"

Scrooge did what he was told, and held it fast. Suddenly they stood in the city streets on Christmas morning, where people were gleefully rushing about, singing carols and greeting each other.

The Spirit led him straight to the house of Scrooge's clerk, and right into the dwelling. Mrs. Cratchit, Bob Cratchit's wife, was dressed poorly in an old gown, but it was brave in ribbons. As young Peter Crachit plunged a fork into a saucepan of potatoes, a smaller Cratchit girl came running in.

"Here's Martha, Mother!" cried the young Cratchit girl.

"Why, bless your heart, how late you are," said Mrs. Cratchit, kissing her and taking off her daughter's shawl and bonnet. "Sit down before the fire, my dear."

"No, no! There's Father coming!" cried the two young Cratchits. "Hide, Martha, hide!"

So Martha hid herself and in came Bob, the father, in his threadbare clothes, with Tiny Tim upon his shoulders. Poor Tiny Tim, he held a little crutch!

"Why, where's our Martha?" cried Bob Cratchit, looking round.

"Not coming," said Mrs. Cratchit.

"Not coming!" said Bob, his spirits sinking, for he had carried Tim home from church on his shoulders as quickly as he could. "Not coming on Christmas Day?"

Martha didn't like to see him disappointed, even as a joke, so she came out from behind a chair and ran into his arms. The two other Cratchits took Tiny Tim off to wash up for dinner.

"And how did little Tim behave?" asked Mrs. Cratchit.

"As good as gold," said Bob, "and better. Somehow he gets thoughtful sitting by himself so much. He told me, coming home, that he liked to ride upon my shoulders because it put him a little closer to heaven." Bob paused. "I think that Tim grows stronger and more hearty every day." Mrs. Cratchit nodded in agreement.

The two young Cratchits returned with Tim and set chairs for everybody, while Martha helped Mrs. Cratchit set the table, crowning the meal with a small goose. Bob put Tiny Tim beside him in a little corner of the table as the others sat down. Grace was said and it was succeeded by a breathless pause, as Mrs. Cratchit plunged the carving knife into the goose. But when she did, a murmur of delight arose all round the board.

There never was such a goose. Its tenderness and flavor, size and cheapness, were the themes of universal admiration. Stretched out by applesauce and mashed potatoes, it was a sufficient dinner for the whole family. But now Mrs. Cratchit—too nervous to bear witnesses—left the room alone to take the pudding from the oven. In half a minute she returned, flushed but smiling proudly, with the pudding hard and firm, blazing in ignited brandy.

"Oh, a wonderful pudding!" Bob Cratchit said. Everybody had something to say about it, but nobody said or thought that it was a very small pudding for such a large family.

At last, Bob Cratchit stood up and raised his glass. "A Merry Christmas to us all, my dears. God bless us!" Which all the family reechoed.

"God bless us every one!" said Tiny Tim, the last of all. Bob held Tim's little hand, as if he wished to keep him by his side, and worried that he might be taken from him.

"Spirit," said Scrooge, with an interest he had never felt before, "tell me if Tiny Tim will live."

"I see a vacant seat," replied the Ghost, "and a crutch without an owner, carefully preserved."

"No, no," said Scrooge. "Oh no, kind Spirit! Say he will be spared."

"If he might die, he had better do it, and decrease the surplus population," said the Spirit.

Scrooge hung his head to hear his own words quoted by the Spirit, and

was overcome with penitence and grief. But he raised his head upon hearing his own name.

"To Mr. Scrooge!" said Bob, lifting his glass once again, "the Founder of the Feast!"

"The Founder of the Feast indeed!" cried Mrs. Cratchit, reddening. "If he were here I'd give him a piece of my mind to feast upon."

"My dear," said Bob, "the children; Christmas Day."

"I'll drink to his health for your sake and the day's," said Mrs. Cratchit, "not for his. Long life to him. A Merry Christmas and a Happy New Year!"

They were a happy family, loving one another, and as Scrooge and the Spirit parted, Scrooge had his eye upon them, and especially on Tiny Tim, until the last.

By now, it was getting dark, as Scrooge and the Spirit continued along the streets. Suddenly Scrooge recognized the voice of his nephew and heard him laugh, and found himself in a bright, gleaming room, with the Spirit standing smiling by his side. Scrooge's niece by marriage laughed as heartily as he, along with their assembled friends.

"He said that Christmas was a humbug, as I live!" cried Scrooge's nephew. "He believed it, too! And he threw this paperweight at me as I left."

"Shame on him, Fred!" said Fred's pretty wife, indignantly.

"He's a comical old fellow," said Scrooge's nephew, "that's the truth; and not so pleasant as he might be. However, his offenses carry their own punishment, and I have nothing to say against him."

"I'm sure he is very rich, Fred," said his wife.

"What does that matter, my dear!" said Scrooge's nephew. "His wealth is of no use to him. He doesn't do any good with it. Who suffers by his ill whims? Himself, always. Here, he takes it into his head to dislike us, and he won't come and dine with us. What's the consequence?"

"He misses a very good dinner," said Fred's wife. Everybody else agreed, for they had certainly enjoyed the dinner.

Fred looked at his wife tenderly. He wanted to say something to convey to his guests the depth of his love for her. "You are," he said, faltering, "altogether so satisfactory."

Soon they listened to some music, and sang and danced together. And after a while they decided to play some games. First there was a game of blindman's buff. And it was quite clear that one of Fred's friends, who fancied a young lady, with a kerchief over his eyes, was not blind at all, as he chased and found her.

Then they played a game called Yes and No, and Scrooge was so taken with it he begged the Ghost to allow him to remain. Scrooge's nephew had to think of a thing and the rest must figure out what, with Fred only answering to their questions "yes" or "no," as the case might be. The questioners soon determined that he was thinking of an animal, a live animal, rather a disagreeable animal, a savage animal, an animal that growled and grunted sometimes, and lived in London and was not a bull or a tiger or a bear. At last a young lady cried out, "I know what it is, Fred! I know what it is! It's your uncle Scrooge!" Which it certainly was.

"He has given us plenty of merriment, I am sure," said Fred, "and it would be ungrateful of us not to drink his health. To Uncle Scrooge, wherever he is!"

"To Uncle Scrooge!" they all cried.

Scrooge had become so light of heart that he was quite touched, and might have thanked them all, had the Spirit not hurried him away. "My life upon this globe is very brief," said the Spirit. "It ends tonight. Hark! The time is drawing near." As he led Scrooge through the poorer parts of town, the chimes were ringing three-quarters past eleven.

"Spirit," said Scrooge, looking intently at the Spirit's robe, "I see something strange protruding from the bottom of your skirt. Is it a foot or a claw?"

"Look here," was the Spirit's sorrowful reply. From the fold of his robe, he brought forth two children. They knelt down at his feet and clung to the outside of his garment. They were a boy and a girl, ragged and pathetic.

Scrooge drew back, appalled. "Spirit, are they yours?" he asked.

"They are Mankind's," said the Spirit, looking down upon them. "This boy is Ignorance. This girl is Want. Beware them both, but most of all beware the boy." Want, the Spirit explained, is a condition the world must suffer, but if ignorance is overcome, then want can be helped.

"Have they no refuge or resource?" cried Scrooge.

"Are there no prisons?" said the Spirit, turning on him once again with his own words. "Are there no workhouses?"

The bell struck twelve.

Scrooge looked about him for the Ghost, but it was gone. At the last stroke, he remembered the prediction of old Jacob Marley, and lifting up his eyes, beheld a solemn Phantom, draped and hooded, coming toward him like a mist along the ground.

OF ALL THE GHOSTS THAT SCROOGE HAD SEEN, THIS WAS THE SCARIEST. The Phantom was shrouded in a deep black garment, which concealed its head, its face, its form, and left nothing visible except one outstretched hand. Scrooge was filled with dread, for the Spirit neither spoke nor moved. "I am in the presence of the Ghost of Christmas Yet to Come?" asked Scrooge.

The Spirit did not answer but pointed onward with its hand.

"You are about to show me shadows of the things that have not happened but will happen in the time before us," Scrooge pursued. "Is that so, Spirit?" The Spirit once more pointed forward, as if in confirmation.

"Ghost of the Future!" Scrooge exclaimed, "I fear you more than any

other I have seen. But because I know your purpose is to do me good, and because I hope to live to be a better man than I was, I am prepared to bear you company, and do it with a thankful heart. Will you not speak to me?"

The Ghost gave no reply.

"Lead on, then!" said Scrooge.

The Spirit moved away in similar silent fashion. Scrooge followed in the shadow of its robe, which carried him along.

The Spirit stopped beside a little knot of businessmen talking on the street. Observing that the hand was pointed to them, Scrooge advanced to listen to their talk.

"No," said a fat man, "I don't know much about it, either way. I only know he's dead."

"When did he die?" inquired another.

"Last night, I believe."

"I thought he'd never die," said a third.

"What has he done with his money?" asked a red-faced gentleman.

"He hasn't left it to me. That's all I know," said the first.

There was a general laugh.

"It's likely to be a cheap funeral," continued the speaker, "for I don't know of anybody who will go to it. Suppose we make up a party and volunteer?"

"I don't mind going if lunch is provided," someone responded. Another laugh.

As the speakers strolled away, Scrooge looked to the Spirit for an explanation, but the Spirit gave him none. They left this scene and went to an obscure part of town, where Scrooge had never been, and he saw some people haggling over the possessions of someone who had died. Scrooge was horrified that the goods they described sounded very much like his own!

The Ghost conducted him through several familiar streets. They entered poor Bob Cratchit's house, and found the mother and the children seated round the fire. They were very quiet. The mother laid her work upon the table and put her hand up to her face. "The work makes my eyes weak by candle-light," she said, "and I wouldn't show weak eyes to your father when he comes home, for all the world. And there is your father at the door!"

She hurried to meet him and Bob came in and sat down. Then the two young Cratchits got upon his knees and each child laid a little cheek against his face.

"You went today, then, Bob?" asked Mrs. Cratchit.

"Yes, my dear," said Bob. "It would have done you good to see how

green a place it is. But you'll go often. I promised him I would walk there on a Sunday. My little, little child!" cried Bob. He broke down crying all at once.

When he had composed himself, they drew around the fire and talked. "However and whenever we part from one another," said Bob, "I am sure we shall none of us forget Tiny Tim, shall we?"

"Never, Father," they all cried.

"Then I am very happy," said Bob, "I am very happy!"

Scrooge wrung his hands. "Spirit," he said, "tell me what man that was that the other men were talking about before?"

The spirit led him to an iron gate. A churchyard. The Spirit stood among the graves, and pointed down to one. Scrooge advanced toward it trembling.

"Before I draw nearer to that one stone to which you point," said Scrooge, "answer me one question. Are these the shadows of the things that will be, or are they shadows of things that may be, only?"

Still the Ghost pointed to the grave by which it stood.

Scrooge crept toward it, trembling as he went, and following the finger, read upon the gravestone his own name, EBENEZER SCROOGE.

"No, Spirit! Oh, no, no! Spirit, hear me! I am not the man I was. I will not continue to be that man. Assure me that I yet may change these shadows you have shown me by altering my life! I will honor Christmas in my heart, and try to keep it all the year. I will live in the Past and the Present and the Future. The Spirits of all Three shall strive within me. I will not shut out the lessons that they teach."

Suddenly the Phantom's hood and robe shrunk, collapsed, and dwindled down into a bedpost.

YES! THE BEDPOST WAS HIS OWN. THE BED WAS HIS OWN, THE ROOM WAS HIS OWN. BEST AND HAPPIEST OF ALL, THE TIME BEFORE HIM WAS HIS OWN, TO MAKE AMENDS IN!

"I will live in the Past, the Present, and the Future!" Scrooge repeated as he scrambled out of bed. "Oh, Jacob Marley! Heaven and Christmastime be praised for this! The shadows of the things that would have been may be dispelled! They will be! I know they will!" He rushed about in every direction.

"I hardly know what to do!" cried Scrooge, laughing and crying in the same breath. "I am as light as a feather, I am as happy as an angel. I am as merry as a schoolboy!"

He heard the church bells ringing out the lustiest peals he had ever heard. "Oh, glorious, glorious!" he cried, looking out the window, giddy with joy. He dressed quickly.

Now, it happens that when Scrooge emerged from his house he called out to me. "What's today, boy?" Little did I know, at that moment, what a great transformation had come over Mr. Ebenezer Scrooge.

"What?" I asked, for I could hardly understand what he might be asking.

"What's today, my fine fellow?" said Scrooge.

"Today," I replied. "Why, it's Christmas Day!"

"Christmas Day!" said Scrooge aloud. "I haven't missed it. The Spirits have done it all in one night. They can do anything they like! Look here, my fine fellow!"

"Yes?" I replied.

"Do you know the poulterer's, in the next street, at the corner?"

"I should hope so," I replied.

"An intelligent boy!" said Scrooge. "A remarkable boy. Do you know whether they've sold the prize turkey that was hanging up there? The big one?"

"What, the one as big as me?" I asked.

"What a delightful boy," said Scrooge. "It's a pleasure to talk to you. Yes, my boy!"

"It's hanging there now," I replied.

"Is it?" said Scrooge. "Go and buy it."

I must have looked strangely at him, for I knew his reputation.

"No, no," said Scrooge, "I am in earnest. Go and buy it and tell the poulterer to bring it here, that I may give him directions where to take it. Come back with him and I'll give you a shilling. Come back with him in less than five minutes and I'll give you half a crown." He almost seemed surprised to hear himself say this. And as I shot off in that direction I heard him say, "I'll send it to Bob Cratchit's."

When I came back with the poulterer, Scrooge said, "Here's the turkey.

Whoop! Hello! How are you! Merry Christmas!"

The poulterer looked at him curiously.

"Why, it's impossible to carry that to Camden Town," he told the poulterer. "You must have a cab." The chuckle with which he said this, and the chuckle with which he paid for the turkey, and the chuckle with which he paid for the cab, and the chuckle with which he paid me, came all at once. Then he took me aside for a little talk.

Scrooge continued down the street and saw the gentlemen who had come into his counting house the day before, asking "Scrooge and Marley's, I believe?"

"My dear sir," said Scrooge, taking one of the gentlemen by the hand, "How do you do? A Merry Christmas to you, sir!"

"Mr. Scrooge?" said the gentleman, puzzled.

"Yes," said Scrooge. "That is my name. And I fear it may not be pleasant to you. I beg your pardon. And may I offer you the following?" Here Scrooge whispered in his ear.

"Lord bless me!" cried the gentleman. "My dear Mr. Scrooge, are you serious?"

"If you please," said Scrooge. "Not a farthing less. A great many back-payments are included in it, I assure you."

"I don't know what to say," said the other, shaking hands with him.

"Don't say anything, please," said Scrooge. "Will you come and see me?"

"I will!" cried the old gentleman.

"Merry Christmas, Mr. Marley," said the other.

He walked about the streets, and watched the people hurrying to and fro, and patted little children on the head, and everything seemed to give him pleasure. He even managed to join in to learn a Christmas carol.

In the afternoon, he turned his steps toward his nephew's house. He knocked at the door, and Fred's wife appeared. "Is my nephew home?" he asked.

She looked quite surprised. Fred called toward the door, "Who's that?"

"It's I. Your uncle Scrooge. I have come to dinner. Will you let me in, Fred?"

Let him in! Fred and his wife made him right at home! What a wonderful party!

He was early at the office the next morning. More than anything, he wanted to be there first, and catch Bob Cratchit coming late!

And he did it. The clock struck nine. No Bob. A quarter past. No Bob. When he finally showed up, he was a full eighteen-and-a-half minutes behind time.

Bob was on his stool in a jiffy, working away with his pen.

"Hello!" growled Scrooge. "What do you mean by coming here at this time of day!"

"I am very sorry, sir," said Bob. "I won't do it again. I was making rather merry yesterday, sir."

"Now, I'll tell you what," said Scrooge. "I am not going to stand this sort of thing any longer. And therefore," he continued, leaping from his stool and looking at Bob sternly: "And therefore I am going to raise your salary! A Merry Christmas, Bob," said Scrooge, as he clapped him on the back. " A merrier

Christmas than I have given you for many a year! Now, make up the fires and buy another coal scuttle's-worth before you dot another 'i', Bob Cratchit!"

I know all this because Scrooge invited me to be his apprentice. "I have much to pass on," he told me, "and not just the business of my trade. What Old Fezziwig tried to teach me was what I failed to learn: the lessons of good will and boundless charity!"

Scrooge was better than his word. He did it all, and infinitely more. And to Tiny Tim, who did *not* die, he was like a second father. He became as good a friend, as good a master, and as good a man, as any city knew in all the world.

And it was always said of him that he knew how to keep Christmas well, if any man alive possessed the knowledge. May that be truly said of all of us! And so, as Tiny Tim observed, God bless us, every one!